MARKED OMEGA

Bear Shifter MM MPreg Romance

Michael Levi

Copyright © 2024 Michael Levi

All rights reserved

The characters and events portrayed in this book are fictitious. Any similarity to real persons, living or dead, is coincidental and not intended by the author.

No part of this book may be reproduced, or stored in a retrieval system, or transmitted in any form or by any means, electronic, mechanical, photocopying, recording, or otherwise, without express written permission of the publisher.

ISBN: 9798878631181
Imprint: Independently published

1st edition

CONTENTS

Title Page	
Copyright	
Chapter 1	1
Chapter 2	6
Chapter 3	11
Chapter 4	16
Chapter 5	21
Chapter 6	26
Chapter 7	31
Chapter 8	36
Chapter 9	41
Chapter 10	46
Chapter 11	51
Chapter 12	56
Bruno's Epilogue	61
Oliver's Epilogue	65
Similar Books	69
About the Author	71

CHAPTER 1

Bruno

I could feel it in the breeze. He was here, my mate. I knew that he was nearby. I sniffed the air in front of me, closing in on his scent. He might or might not be aware of my presence. It didn't matter.

I crept forward behind the bushes, vaguely aware that I was naked. I was in my natural habitat, so no reason to worry about me being naked.

I was thirty-five years old and I was still looking for my fated mate. That was the reason why my heart was galloping like a wild horse. I was only thinking about finding this mate of mine and finally having the life I had always wanted, even though it was going to be short-lived.

I proceeded forward, pushing through the bushes before finding a small downward slope. This part of the forest had a small lake, and in it, there was a person. Or rather, I should say that there was a wolf.

Even from afar, just from his scent, I could tell that he was a wolf. A pretty wolfie with black hair, black eyes, and a skin so white that it shone brightly under the sunlight.

My ears perked up. I could hear what he was mumbling to himself. "Fucking bullshit. I can't believe that my friends threw horse shit on me, and I'm on vacation. I'm supposed to be enjoying my time here, but I'm not really. I don't even like the water and here I am bathing myself."

I chuckled. Little wolfie didn't like the water? That was funny. He was in his human form, so there should be no problem with that.

I proceeded forward, my mind focused solely on the fact that he was my fated mate. We shifters always knew our fated mates the moment that we spotted them for the first time, and now was no different.

In that moment, his ears perked up, most likely hearing my footsteps. I wasn't trying to hide, so finding out that I was lurking around him wasn't a difficult thing to do.

But it did make him blush. He immediately put his hands in front of his crotch, trying to hide his cock. I chuckled. Why do something like that when I couldn't even see his cock? It was underwater.

"What are you trying to hide, little wolfie?" I asked, a sly smile spreading across my face.

"It's none of your business." His eyes widened. "Plus, you shouldn't be naked. That's not allowed here in the oasis."

I cackled. "Little wolfie, I don't know anything about that. I didn't read the manual before coming here."

"There is no manual. It's just something that everybody knows."

"Well, clearly, I didn't know."

And at the same time, he couldn't stop his eyes from moving down. He was aware that my eyes were up here, and he couldn't stop looking down. Suffice it to say that he thought that my cock was big and impressive.

And I wasn't even semi-hard.

I proceeded forward and he immediately said with a bit more energy than before. "Don't come any closer! I'm just taking a bath."

"I know that's what you're doing, little wolfie, but I'm also aware that you think exactly the same way I do. You can feel the same thing I feel, don't you?"

Even though it was difficult for him to admit something like that, his arousal was more than evident. He nodded slowly, his hands moving away from his crotch.

I was lying before that I couldn't see his dick underwater. I could see a glimpse of it, but it was deformed because of the light refraction in the water. That was okay. He was my fated mate and we would have so many more opportunities to see each other more intimately.

"Which means it's okay for me to step forward and join you in the water." I paused. "Are you going to stop me from doing that, little wolfie?"

He shook his head and said, "No, I'm not going to do that, but I want you to stop calling me 'little wolfie.' First, I'm not little, and second and last, my name is Oliver."

My smile widened. "All right, Oliver. I just want to get close to you, feel you, and see what happens after that."

He allowed me to get into the water. It was cool and refreshing, a stark contrast to the hot sunlight. And I moved through it toward the little omega. I dwarfed him and that might even be an understatement.

I didn't think too much about it. I enjoyed being bigger than omegas like him.

When we were close enough, my nostrils and my lungs were filled by his scent. With my heart racing the way that it was, I couldn't help but feel more and more that he was my destined one.

He sighed and asked, "So, what's going to happen now? I gave you my name and you didn't even tell me yours."

"Just call me Bruno."

"Bruno… Okay."

There was a moment of silence until he finally mentioned, "You look scary and way older than me."

"Sheesh, Oliver. No need to bring that up. I know that my time is running out."

He was aware that we shifters had limited time to find our fated mates.

He chuckled and said, "Okay, and what is going to happen now exactly? Are we going to fuck?"

I smiled again. "Something like that. We can do it in two ways. I can do it now right here in this lake or we can do it later after we know a little bit more about each other. What do you want, Oliver?"

He bit his bottom lip, considering both options. Both were tempting. "I feel something different for you as well, Bruno."

He put his hand on my chest, caressing it. "We're not going to fuck, but we are going to taste a little bit of each other," he continued.

And by saying that, I knew exactly what he meant.

My heart raced as Oliver's words sank in. He wanted to taste me, and I couldn't resist the temptation. I leaned in, closing the distance between our heads, and pressed my lips to his. His lips were soft and inviting, and I could feel the electricity between us.

Oliver's hands moved to my shoulders, pulling me closer as our kiss deepened. I could feel his tongue against mine, and it sent a shiver down my spine. I wrapped my arms around him, holding him tightly as we lost ourselves in the moment.

We broke apart for a moment, both of us panting and gasping for breath. Oliver looked up at me, his eyes filled with desire, and I knew that I wanted more. I leaned in again, kissing him harder this time.

Our bodies moved together, and I could feel the heat radiating off of him. I ran my hands down his back, feeling the muscles tense beneath my touch. He moaned softly into my mouth, and it sent a jolt of pleasure through me.

I could feel my cock growing harder with each passing moment, and I knew that I couldn't resist the temptation for much longer. I pulled away from Oliver, looking down at him with a hungry gaze.

He looked up at me, his eyes filled with lust. "So, what now?" He asked, his voice barely above a whisper.

I didn't waste any time answering. I reached down, pulling him up onto his feet. Oliver wrapped his legs around me, and I carried him to the edge of the lake. I laid him down on the soft grass, looking down at him with a fierce desire.

I ran my hands over his body, feeling every inch of him. He was perfect in every way, and I couldn't wait to explore every inch of him. I leaned down, kissing his neck and chest as I made my way lower.

Oliver moaned softly as I reached his cock, already hard and ready for me. I took it in my hand, feeling the weight of it. I leaned down, taking the tip into my mouth and tasting him for the first time.

Oliver groaned, his hands gripping the grass beneath him as I moved my mouth up and down his shaft. I could feel him growing harder with each passing moment, and I knew that I was driving him wild.

I moved my hand to his balls, massaging them gently as I continued to suck on his cock. Oliver's moans grew louder, and I could feel him tensing beneath me. I knew that he was close, and I wasn't going to stop until he came.

With one final thrust of my mouth, Oliver exploded, his cum filling my mouth. I swallowed it down eagerly, savoring the taste of him. Oliver lay there panting, his eyes closed as I pulled away from him.

I looked down at him, a satisfied smile on my face. Oliver opened his eyes, looking up at me with a dazed expression. "That was amazing," he said, his voice still shaky.

I leaned down, kissing him deeply. "It was just the beginning," I whispered, my voice filled with promise.

CHAPTER 2

Oliver

It was amazing. Better than I thought it was going to be, to be honest. When I was old enough to understand what being a shifter really meant, I thought that it was all bullshit, but one of the reasons for that was because I was living mostly with humans. I even had high school with them, so of course I didn't believe in love at first sight.

But it was really different with us shifters. When we found our fated mate, everything was different. Our bodies reacted differently. We knew from that moment on that our lives were going to be different.

And here this was happening right here in the Oasis for Bears. I didn't think that it was going to happen here of all places.

Bruno confirmed everything after what he did. I could still feel the aftershocks traveling through my body. Never before did someone make me feel so much pleasure in such a short time.

I was only twenty years old. I was in college now and the only thing I was thinking about was how to link my college career to my professional one down the line. I wasn't thinking about finding the love of my life.

But it appeared that everything changed for the better.

He put his head on his hand, his elbow on the grass, and he was looking at me. His sly smile didn't disappear from his face. "What do you say, Oliver? That really was amazing, wasn't it?"

I blushed. It was amazing. I wanted more right now. But, having grown up among humans, I was still mostly like them, and if there was one thing that they taught me, it was that, first, I should find out more about the person that I was 'dating.'

This was really it. I was dating this bear and we should learn more about each other.

I should start by asking him, "Bruno, what are you doing here? Why did you come to the oasis?"

His eyes darkened for a brief second as if he was considering changing his initial answer, but then, his eyes immediately cleared up. "Probably for the same reason you came here, Oliver. Just to kick back and enjoy myself. If you're wondering, no I didn't come here thinking that I was going to find you."

My heart warmed up. It made me feel good that he found me completely by accident. Maybe the thing about destiny actually being a thing was true. Maybe it really existed.

In any case, I wasn't going to focus too much on that.

I was going to focus more on finding out more about Bruno. He was exciting, alluring, and he made me want to know everything about him.

"And what do you do for a living?"

He chuckled. "Oliver, is this some kind of interrogation? Because it sure feels like that."

I chuckled as well. "No, it's not an interrogation. If we are to live together for the rest of our lives, then I need to know everything about you."

His finger dabbed the tip of my nose, making shivers run down my spine. "Right here and now, really? I think we should take things slow."

"You may be right about that, but you're not going to get away from answering that question."

He sighed. "I'm retired."

My eyes widened. "You are retired? What? That doesn't make any sense. You can't be more than forty years old."

He chuckled. "You really think that I'm that old?"

I blushed. "No, I was just saying that you are too young to be retired."

He looked at the sky. Maybe he was admiring the beautiful shade of blue and the clouds. "Yeah, I'm too young for that. I'm retired for another reason."

My heart raced. He was showing me more and more about him, and I was curious. I just wanted to find out everything about this potential lifelong partner of mine.

At the same moment, I was already wondering what it was going to be like when I was pregnant with his cub and we would have a family.

Where would we even live? I had no idea. I didn't plan that far ahead in my life yet.

So many questions and so few answers.

I caressed his right peck, making his eyes look down there and then back at me. "Well, are you going to tell me why you retired so early?"

He exhaled, still looking at the sky. He looked pensive. "I shouldn't."

I sat up, my eyes widening. "You are not going to tell me something so simple about your life? Really? I don't understand, Bruno. You came here telling me that I'm your fated mate and now you're holding back something like that from me?"

He sat up as well, putting his arm around my shoulders and bringing me closer to his body. "The reason is simple, Oliver. You will find out about that when I think that you deserve it."

I couldn't help but groan. I didn't think that he was going to play with my thoughts like this, making me wonder what he was really doing before retiring.

"And you still think that I am your fated mate, right?"

He chuckled. "I just don't think that. I know you are."

I shook my head, a tightlipped smile on my face. "All right, Bruno. What do you want to do now with your *fated mate*?"

His eyes raked over my body. "I think I know exactly what I want to do with you. Ready for it?"

He stood up and my eyes couldn't stop staring at his immense cock. Mine didn't hold a candle to it. That was how different it was from anything I had seen before.

I stood up as well, noticing once again that he towered over me. The top of my head reached his shoulders and no more than that.

As the sunlight continued to filter through the canopies, Bruno led me toward the shimmering water of the lake, a mischievous smile playing on his lips. The anticipation of what awaited me sent a tingling sensation through every inch of my body. I followed willingly, my heart pounding with excitement.

"I'm going to bathe you now, Oliver. I overheard you grumbling about your friends throwing horse shit on you. Some friends you have."

We waded into the cool, refreshing embrace of the lake, its gentle ripples caressing our bare skin. Bruno's strong arms enveloped me, pulling me closer, as he guided me to a shallower part of the water. The sensation of his touch against my skin sent shivers of desire coursing through me.

With a tender yet commanding presence, Bruno gently guided me to lower myself into the water, ensuring my comfort and ease. The coolness of the liquid enveloped my body, soothing my skin and awakening my senses. He stood behind me, his body pressed close, his hands resting gently on my shoulders.

I closed my eyes, allowing myself to fully surrender to the experience. Bruno's touch was like a gentle caress, his hands gliding down my arms, tracing the curve of my waist, and finally settling on my hips. The warmth of his touch radiated through me, sparking a fire deep within.

He leaned in, his lips delicately brushing against the back of my neck, sending shivers of pleasure down my spine. His breath, warm and inviting, teased my senses, heightening my anticipation. Slowly, he began to pour water over me, the liquid cascading down my body, cleansing and arousing me simultaneously.

With each gentle pour, Bruno's hands followed, his touch like a sensual dance upon my skin. The water mingled with the curves of my body, accentuating every contour, every sensitive spot. His fingers traced delicate circles, showing how much he knew of what he was doing.

As the water streamed over me, Bruno's touch became more deliberate, his hands gliding over my pecs, tracing the swell of my hips, and exploring the softness of my thighs. His touch was both tender and possessive, his fingertips leaving a trail of sensation that made me ache for more.

He moved even closer, his body aligning with mine, his chest pressing against my back. I could feel the heat of his breath against my ear as he murmured things I couldn't make out. The intimacy of the moment was overwhelming, the connection between us deepening with every touch.

With a slow and deliberate motion, Bruno cupped his hands, gathering water and pouring it over my hair. The cool liquid ran through my locks, caressing my scalp and washing away any lingering tension. His fingers massaged my scalp, awakening my senses and relaxing me further.

As he continued to bathe me, his attention shifted to my face, his touch gentle and reverent. He traced the contours of my cheeks, his thumbs brushing lightly against my lips. I parted them slightly, inviting him in, and he obliged, his fingers exploring the softness and moistness within.

The water continued to flow, cleansing and purifying us both, stripping away any inhibitions and leaving only raw desire in its wake. Bruno's touch, his attentiveness, made me feel cherished as if our souls were merging in this intimate act of care and devotion.

As the bathing ritual came to an end, Bruno pulled me into his embrace once more, his body providing warmth and solace. The water dripped from our bodies, mingling with the desires that still lingered in the air. We stood there, in the embrace of the lake, the world around us fading away.

At the end, I said, "Thanks. That was really so good."

CHAPTER 3

Bruno

After bathing Oliver, we decided that it was best to lie down on the grass to dry our bodies. I was wet, too. So, we lay down on the grass and we both were looking at the sky, just seeing the clouds drifting.

His hand grabbed mine, squeezing it. "That really was so amazing, Bruno."

"I know, Oliver. It really was. That's why I said we are meant for each other. It would never have happened if we weren't."

"You're right."

We stayed like that for a few minutes, eventually turning our bodies so that our backs could be dried as well. It was a heartwarming moment that I never had with anyone else.

We finished doing that and we stood up. He went for his clothes, which were nearby in a pile. I couldn't help but chuckle. "I'm going around with you naked and you are going to put on your clothes, really?"

"Yes, of course I'm going to put them on. I'm not going to walk around the island naked."

I approached him from behind, a sly smile on my face. "Oliver, you know that ever since coming here, I took off my clothes and never looked back."

"But I'm not like you."

He was blushing and I proceeded to squeeze his ass. He gasped, but there was a smile on his face. "Oliver, you are so shy."

"I know," he said before putting on his underwear and his shorts. Then, he put on his shirt.

"Nothing wrong with that, but it's something that I plan to change about you."

He didn't say anything about that and we proceeded away from the lake. In that moment, I asked, "What about your 'friends'? Shouldn't we do something about them because they threw horseshit at you?"

He hesitated for a moment, his eyes looking right into mine. Then, they looked away. "I don't know. I don't think I want to do anything."

I put my hands on my waist. "You don't want to do anything about the people who did that to you?"

He looked at my eyes again, noticing the seriousness in my stare.

I grabbed his hand, leading him farther away from the lake. "Come on, Oliver. Show me where your 'friends' are and we are going to have a talk about what happened. Ain't no way that I'm letting them get away with what they did."

He made me stop and said with urgency, "But you have no idea who they are. What if they…?"

"What if they what? Hurt me?" I threw my head up, laughing out loud. "I think that it's them who should be worried about me."

He came to me in a hurry, grabbing my arms. "You're not going to hurt them, are you? I don't want to see anybody getting hurt."

I ruffled his hair. "Don't worry, my sweet, sweet omega. I'm not going to hurt anybody."

Then, he let go of my arms. "You promise?"

"Oliver, of course I promise. I may look scary, but I don't hurt people."

He sighed and we proceeded toward where everybody was. Some people looked at me because I was naked, but most ignored me. Things were changing here in the oasis.

"All right, Oliver. Tell me where your friends are."

He pointed his finger toward a group of people playing beach soccer on one of the beaches.

"Ahh, so it's them. I'm going to make sure they understand it's not okay to hurt you."

"I just hope they don't try to hurt you."

I chuckled. "If they try something like that, they are going to be the ones sorry that it happened."

We proceeded toward that group of people. They were so engrossed in playing beach soccer that they didn't notice us coming. Didn't notice Oliver coming, either. Like I said before, *some friends he had.*

With my hands on my waist, I said very loudly, "Hey, you guys. Is it true that you dumped horse shit on Oliver?"

Everybody that was playing beach soccer finally stopped doing so, looking at me. Their eyes widened immediately. Most of them couldn't stop looking at my cock. It was a funny moment, but I remained serious.

"And you are?" One of them asked.

"You can call me Bruno. I'm here because you hurt your supposed friend."

Everybody then glanced at Oliver. "Oliver, who the hell is this guy?" Somebody else asked.

"He is my mate."

Their jaws dropped open. "Your mate? Seriously? You came here to the oasis with us and you think that we are going to believe you found your mate right here and not on the mainland when you were actively looking for one?"

Oliver was going to say something, but I interrupted. "What do you know about finding your mate? Have you found yours already?"

The same guy from before immediately opened his mouth, but he realized he didn't have anything to say. He only mumbled something - something that I didn't care to understand or make out.

"Yeah, I was right about that. You don't know anything about finding your mate. None of you do, in fact."

Nobody challenged me about that.

I took a few steps forward so that I was closer to the one I was talking to. Staring straight into his eyes, I demanded, "You're all going to say you are sorry about what you did to Oliver."

His lips trembled, but he still said, "I'm not going to do that. I don't have to. You can't demand anything from me. If anything, you should be arrested for being completely naked here. It's not permitted."

I chuckled. "I wonder who is going to do that. Is somebody going to do it? Because I don't see anybody coming here to arrest me."

He looked around as if waiting for somebody to appear and apprehend me, but nobody was going to do that. Even though the place had guards, they were not going to cause a ruckus. What happened before in the oasis left a scar in this place.

He exhaled and proceeded toward Oliver. "I'm sorry about what we did, Oliver."

The rest followed suit, saying that they were sorry about what they did.

Oliver reacted the way I thought he was going to. He didn't say anything and appeared to be embarrassed by the whole thing.

But it was okay to be embarrassed. In a few days from now, he was going to look back at this moment and think how thankful he was that it happened.

After we were finished with that, I turned to Oliver and said, "Okay, Oliver. Time to leave."

As we proceeded away from his group of friends, I asked, "And for what reason did they dump manure on you?"

And I also couldn't help but wonder how there were even horses in the oasis. I'd never seen them, to be honest.

"Because I suck at playing beach soccer. They got furious at me and decided to take out their frustration on me."

Tears pricked his eyes and I immediately put my hands on his shoulders, forcing him to look into my eyes. "Hey, Oliver. Don't worry about that. It's just beach soccer. Nothing to fret over."

He wiped the tears coming from the corners of his eyes. "You're right about that, Bruno. Thanks for supporting me."

I put my arm around his shoulders and said, "So, where's your room?"

He blushed. "What do you think you are going to do when you are in my room with me and alone?"

I kissed his cheek. "Something special, my sweet little Omega."

He slapped my shoulder playfully. "I'm not little, like I said."

"Sure, whatever you say, Oliver."

We proceeded toward his room in the hotel. He opened the door and we stepped inside. My eyes scanned the surroundings. There was nothing important in here.

It was just his room, we were alone, and my bear was raging within me.

CHAPTER 4

Bruno

I couldn't help myself anymore. My body was screaming for his touch, and I knew he felt the same way. I turned to him and pulled him close, our bodies pressed tightly together. My heart was pounding in my chest as I leaned in and captured his lips in a passionate kiss.

He moaned softly against me, his body trembling with desire. I deepened the kiss, my tongue exploring his mouth as my hands roamed over his body. I could feel every muscle, every curve, and it only made me want him more.

I broke the kiss and pulled back, looking into his eyes. They were filled with lust and longing, and it made me feel alive. I reached down and started to slowly lift his shirt, revealing his toned abs and chest. I ran my fingers over his skin, feeling the goosebumps rise as I traced circles around his nipples.

He let out a soft gasp as I leaned down and placed a gentle kiss on his chest, my tongue darting out to taste his skin. I could feel his heart pounding beneath my lips, and it only made me more excited. I continued to kiss and nibble my way down his chest, making my way toward his shorts.

I hooked my fingers into the waistband of his shorts and started to slowly pull them down, revealing his hard length. I couldn't help but let out a low growl as I took in the sight of him.

He was perfect in every way.

I pulled his shorts all the way off and then turned my attention to his underwear. I hooked my fingers into the waistband and slowly pulled them down as well, taking my time to savor every inch of his body that was revealed to me.

Once his underwear was off, I took a step back and admired him. He was completely naked and vulnerable, and it only made me want him more. I stepped forward and took him in my hand, stroking him gently as I leaned in and captured his lips in another passionate kiss.

He moaned into my mouth as I continued to stroke him, my other hand roaming over his body. I could feel his muscles tensing as I brought him closer and closer to the edge. I knew he was close, and I couldn't wait to feel him release.

I broke the kiss and looked into his eyes, my hand still moving up and down his shaft. He was panting heavily, his eyes squeezed shut as he fought to hold back his orgasm. I leaned in and whispered in his ear, "Come for me, Oliver. I want to feel you come all over my face."

He let out a low groan and his body tensed, his muscles straining as he finally reached his peak. I felt his warmth spill over my hand and onto my face, and I couldn't help but let out a moan of my own. It was the most incredible feeling, knowing that I had brought him to this point.

I continued to stroke him through his orgasm, my hand covered in his come. I leaned in and placed a gentle kiss on his lips, tasting myself on him. He wrapped his arms around me and pulled me close, holding me tightly as he caught his breath.

We stood there for a few moments, our bodies pressed together as we reveled in the aftermath of our passion. I could feel his heart pounding against my chest, and it made me feel alive.

As we pulled apart, I looked up at him and smiled. "That was incredible," I said, my voice husky with desire.

He returned my smile and leaned in to place a gentle kiss on my lips. "It was," he agreed. "But we're not done yet."

I grinned, feeling a surge of excitement course through my

veins. Oliver's words sent a delicious shiver down my spine. I reached down, my hand gliding along his thigh, caressing his soft skin as I made my way to his tight, untouched asshole.

Then, I made him bend over.

With a teasing smile, I gently pressed my index finger against his entrance, feeling the resistance and the anticipation building between us. Oliver gasped, his eyes widening as I applied a bit of pressure, slowly easing my finger inside him.

His body tensed, but I reassured him with a soft kiss on his lips and whispered, "Relax, baby." I moved my finger in a circular motion, gradually exploring the tightness of his ass, relishing in the way his body responded to my touch.

Oliver's moans grew louder, his hips instinctively pushing back against my finger, urging me to go deeper. I obliged, adding a second finger, feeling him stretch and yield to my touch. His walls clenched around me, a delicious mix of pleasure and slight discomfort.

As I continued to finger him, I leaned in close, my lips brushing against his ear. "You feel so incredible, Oliver," I whispered. "I love the way you tremble under my touch, the way your body yields to me."

Oliver's breath hitched. His back arched, inviting me to explore further, to make him feel things he never thought possible. I obliged, my fingers curling inside him, searching for that sweet spot that would make him lose control.

And when I found it, Oliver cried out, his voice echoing through the room. I quickened the pace, my fingers delving deeper, hitting that spot repeatedly until he was a writhing mess beneath me. The sounds he made only made me hornier.

With my free hand, I reached around and found his throbbing cock, stroking it in time with my movements inside him. The sensations overwhelmed him, his body trembling with ecstasy as he moaned my name, his pleasure mingling with the raw desire that consumed us both.

As his climax approached, I leaned in, my lips brushing against his ear once more. "Come for me, Oliver," I whispered. "I want to feel you explode yet again."

And with those words, Oliver succumbed to the pleasure, his body convulsing in orgasmic bliss. His release coated my hand, mingling with the slickness of his ass, and I reveled in the sheer intensity of the moment.

It wasn't at all surprising that he came twice in a row. That was another fruit of the fact that we were fated mates.

"That really was amazing, Bruno," he said, sounding breathless.

"I know, my sweet Omega. And you know what's going to happen now?"

"I'm going to knot you, Oliver. You know that this is what happens when two mates find each other."

He nodded and agreed. He knew that it was always going to happen. It might as well happen now.

I was behind him, my hard length pressing against his entrance. I could feel his body tense as he prepared for the invasion, but I reassured him with soft whispers and gentle caresses. I lined myself up and began to push inside, feeling the resistance of his body as it struggled to accommodate my size.

Oliver let out a soft whimper as I entered him, his body tensing as I slowly inched my way inside. I could feel every muscle, every ripple of his body as it stretched to accommodate me. It was an incredible feeling, knowing that I was the one causing him so much pleasure and pain.

As I continued to push myself deeper, Oliver let out a low moan, his body trembling as he adjusted to my size. I could feel his muscles relax as he got used to the feeling of me inside him, and it only made me more excited. I began to move my hips, slowly at first, but gradually increasing my pace as I felt him loosen up.

Oliver let out a gasp as I began to thrust in and out of him, my hard length sliding in and out of his tight hole. It was an incredible feeling, one that I had never experienced before. I could feel every inch of him, and it only made me want him more.

The base of my shaft welled, signaling the knot that I was forming in him.

I reached around and took hold of his hard length, stroking him in time with my thrusts. He let out a soft moan as I touched him, his body trembling as I brought him closer and closer to the edge. I could feel his muscles tightening, his body tensing, and I got ready to come inside.

As I continued to thrust in and out of him, I could feel my own orgasm building. I knew that I wasn't going to last much longer, and I could feel the pressure building inside me. I leaned in and whispered in his ear, "I'm going to come inside you, Oliver. I want to fill you up with my seed just as it's meant to happen."

He let out a low moan, his body trembling as I continued to thrust in and out of him. I could feel him getting closer and closer to the edge, and I knew that it was only a matter of time before he came as well.

With one final thrust, I reached my peak. I let out a loud moan as I released inside him, my seed filling him up as I continued to thrust in and out. I could feel his muscles tightening around me, milking every last drop from my body as I came.

As I pulled out, I could feel my seed spilling out of him, coating my length as I slowly pulled away. I looked down at him, my eyes filled with desire as I saw the way his body trembled with pleasure. I leaned in and placed a gentle kiss on his lips, savoring the taste of him as I enjoyed the aftermath of our sex.

CHAPTER 5

Oliver

My eyes fluttered open, thinking about the moment I just had with Bruno. He knotted me. I mean, I knew it was going to happen, but now my life was set. If before I was thinking that I was going to finish college and find a boring job, sitting behind a desk and replying to emails or filling out Excel tables, now everything was different.

I was most likely already pregnant with his seed. And even though this happened in less than a day, I knew that it was the right thing for me. I knew that so well because my heart was warm with love.

I just wanted to be by his side no matter what.

This was what was like for us shifters. Things were wild and fast after finding our mates, even though we didn't even know much about each other. Love at first sight. The humans didn't believe in that anymore, but it certainly happened to us shifters, and it was amazing.

His eyes fluttered open slightly as well, and he groaned, stretching his arms. He put an arm around my shoulders and neck, pulling me closer. I could feel the beating of his heart, and it was soothing, to say the least.

Bruno planted a kiss on my cheek and whispered, "Good night, Oliver."

It was 'good night' because outside was dark and we could see the moonlight filtering through the window. Everything was so hectic that we had sex when it was still daytime and we slept through the whole day.

My stomach rumbled. I was hungry to eat something.

He must've heard that too for he immediately placed his hand on my stomach, stroking it. "Wanna eat something?" He asked.

I answered, "No, not yet. Just want to stay with you, feel you, and maybe even ask some questions about you."

He smiled. "You must have grown up with humans around you. Sometimes, you really act just like them."

"I did, yeah. I didn't have many other shifters around me when I was growing up. It must be the reason why I never felt like I fit in with my 'friends'."

He chuckled. "That's an understatement. If they were really your friends, they would never have dumped manure on you."

"You're right. They were never my friends. I'm just sad that it took me so long to finally acknowledge that."

"It took you too long, honey, but what's important is that you are here with me."

I snuggled up to him, my face resting on his chest. "Yeah, now I'm here with you, Bruno, and you are still a mystery to me."

He chuckled. "You really are funny, Oliver. What else do you want to know about me?"

"Like, uh, where... Did you grow up?"

"I grew up far away from any human civilization. You must know from my accent that it's not very natural. I learned English after I turned eighteen and decided that I had to go far away from the shifter lands to find my mate. Plus, I'm very adventurous. I just wanted something different for my life other than settling down there near my parents' den. It would be boring."

I contemplated his answer, realizing that he told me the truth. At least about that, he didn't have any reason to lie to me.

"That's really interesting. You must have seen so much of the world."

He sighed. "No, not really. I mean, I did see a lot, but I wish that

I had seen even more."

My fingers played with his nipple, making him smile again. "But you can, especially with me. You can show me what you've seen and we can go beyond that. We can take a plane to Europe. It would be amazing."

He kissed me on my lips. "I know, my sweet Omega. It would be amazing."

And yet, I couldn't help but notice that there was a hint of sadness in his eyes. I didn't know why, but it was there and I wasn't one to keep myself from probing further.

"Why are you sad?"

He glanced at me, his eyes growing even sadder. "I'm not sad."

I scowled slightly. "Yes, you are, Bruno. Don't lie to me. If you want us to work, then you have to tell me everything."

His thumb brushed my cheek. "We are going to work; I just know it. It's how it happens with us shifters."

I exhaled. It appeared that he wasn't going to tell me why he was sad and I didn't know if I could change his mind right now. Maybe it was impossible.

In either case, I had something more important to do right now. My stomach was still rumbling.

He got off the bed with me and said, "Time to find something for us to eat, Oliver. Should we hunt in the woods?"

My heart sped up. Living with humans, I didn't know what hunting was really like. We always had cooks to prepare the meals for us. I never really had days where I was the shifter that I was. Sure, sometimes I shifted into my wolf form, but I never hunted.

I nodded and Bruno shifted into a massive brown bear, while I transformed into a sleek gray wolf. Together, we sniffed the air, picking up the scent of a nearby wild boar. Bruno let out a low growl, signaling that he had found our prey.

We stalked through the woods, our senses heightened in our animal forms. The moonlight filtered through the trees, casting eerie shadows on the forest floor. I could hear the sound of the boar crashing through the underbrush, and my heart raced with excitement.

"Are you sure you're ready for this, Oliver?" Bruno asked, his voice deep and rumbling in his bear form. But his mouth didn't move. He spoke to me using his mind only.

"I'm ready," I replied, my voice confident and strong. "Let's do this." I didn't use my mouth either. Didn't have to.

Bruno and I worked together seamlessly, closing in on the boar from opposite sides. When the moment was right, I lunged forward, sinking my teeth into the boar's hindquarters. Bruno moved in quickly, swiping his massive paw and delivering a fatal blow.

We dragged the boar back to a campsite, where Bruno had already built a roaring bonfire. He shifted back into his human form and began to expertly skin and butcher the animal, while I watched in awe.

"Have you ever done this before?" I asked, as Bruno skillfully removed the meat from the bone.

He shook his head. "No, but I've watched my father do it many times. It's an important skill for a shifter to have."

Once the meat was cooked to perfection, we sat down to eat, the warmth of the fire and the taste of the meat filling us with satisfaction.

"This is delicious," I said, savoring the tender, juicy meat.

Bruno grinned. "I'm glad you like it. Hunting and cooking our own food is a tradition among bear shifters. It's a way to connect with nature and our animal instincts."

As we ate, Bruno told me stories of his travels and the places he had seen. He spoke of the beauty of the world beyond the shifter lands, and I couldn't help but feel a sense of longing. I had never left the small town where I grew up, and I was eager to explore the world with Bruno by my side.

"Have you ever been to Japan?" I asked.

He shook his head. "Haven't gone there either, but I've seen plenty of what America has to offer."

"I've always wanted to go there," I admitted. "I'd love to see Kabukicho and Mount Fuji."

Bruno smiled. "We'll go there together, Oliver. I promise."

We finished our meal and sat in companionable silence, watching the flames dance and flicker. Bruno put his arm around me, pulling me close, and I rested my head on his shoulder. In that moment, I knew that our lives were going to be filled with love, adventure, and happiness.

"Thank you, Bruno," I said softly. "For everything."

He turned to me, his eyes filled with warmth and tenderness. "You don't have to thank me, Oliver. It's my pleasure to be with you and to provide for you."

I smiled, feeling a sense of peace and contentment that I had never experienced before. Bruno was my mate, my partner, and my protector. Together, we would face whatever challenges came our way, and we would always have each other's backs.

As the fire died down and the night grew late, Bruno and I curled up together under a blanket of stars. I knew that tomorrow would bring new adventures and challenges, but for now, I was content to be in the arms of the man I loved, surrounded by the beauty of the wilderness.

CHAPTER 6

Bruno

I was carrying Oliver in my arms. I had to take him back to the hotel. He was sleeping soundly as if nothing unusual was happening, and to him, it might really be the case. But to me, everything was about to change.

I didn't come here to the oasis just to kick back and relax. No, I came here for something more important. I had a mission, something that I only could do.

I didn't know if I could pull it off, but I was going to give my best, especially now that I found my mate.

Oliver stirred slightly as if he was going to wake up, but he didn't. Thank goodness. We were proceeding out of the jungle and we were going to his hotel. I was going to take him back to his room so he could sleep soundly in his bed. It was the least he deserved after giving me such an unforgettable day.

He was surprisingly light in my arms, or maybe I was just accustomed to carrying heavy things from one place to the other.

But that wasn't even the most important aspect of this moment. The most important thing was that he looked like an angel in my arms, and he was so cute and lovely.

I couldn't imagine myself living the rest of my life with anybody else. It was also for that reason I knew he was the one.

I took a deep breath, holding back a tear. Come on, I wasn't going to cry right now. We weren't going to be seeing each other for a while, but it was going to be okay.

I could feel how tight my heart was getting and it was because I didn't want to spend any time away from Oliver. He really was my mate and now he was even pregnant with my cub.

He was proud of it too. I could see that in his eyes.

After what felt like an eternity, I finally reached his hotel. During this entire time and before I met him, I was doing some recon on a particular target in the oasis.

His name was Brutus Thornclaw, the president of the Council of Shifters. It was a position of privilege and he was obviously a privileged person from the moment he was born. He was sixty-five years old and a fat bastard.

The things that he did in office couldn't be summarized without diminishing the importance of the side effects they had on our society.

He was one of the reasons why relations between wolf and bear shifters were deteriorating in the past. It was a good thing that things were turning around in that regard, but it didn't change the fact he made a lot of people suffer, even some powerful ones.

That was the reason why I was hired to kill him. It had to be here. His guard was down here, probably thinking that nobody was going to come for him in this place. After all, this place was for relaxation and peace. Not to mention that he didn't even bring many guards with him.

To get to him wasn't going to be easy, but for a merc like me, I could do it, especially because the American government promised a cure for me.

Without it, I wasn't going to live much longer and I certainly wouldn't be able to grow old with Oliver. He gave me another strong reason to finish this job.

I put him down in his bed and he curled up slightly. Then, I draped his body with a blanket and I proceeded to put on some clothes.

In other circumstances, I wouldn't be doing this, but I also didn't want anybody wondering why I was naked. There was no need to bring more attention to me than I already did.

Brutus Thornclaw was located in a villa far away from here. Perhaps it was destiny that was helping me. I was planning to do this assignment quietly, but things could get ugly quickly.

All I knew was that the American government was going to be waiting for me in one of the docks. Then, they would take me to the mainland and I would receive the treatment that I needed.

I had... *brain cancer* and even though they had state-of-the-art technology to cure it, they told me that it might not be enough.

They told me it was going to be risky, but they also promised me that my chances were good and that I was going to be awake in about a few days, if everything happened without complications. A few weeks tops.

It was difficult for me to say this to Oliver, especially because the first thing he was going to think after waking up was that I ghosted him, even though that wasn't the case.

I left a small note on the nightstand by the side of his bed. My text was brief, but Oliver was going to understand. He understood me so well.

I opened the door, looking at Oliver one last time because I didn't know when the next time would be. Then, I proceeded all the way to the other side of the island, looking for Brutus Thornclaw.

He had to be in his room. After all, I had been studying his routine for a long time and I knew that, around this time, he was in his room.

As I closed the distance between me and Brutus' villa, I could hear the sound of laughter and clinking glasses coming from inside. I quickly assessed the situation and found two guards stationed at the entrance. I took a deep breath and stealthily approached them, taking them down swiftly with my bare hands. I had to be quick and quiet, not wanting to alert anyone inside.

I cautiously entered the villa, my senses on high alert. I could hear Brutus' voice coming from a room down the hall. I approached the door, my heart pounding in my chest. This was it.

I kicked the door open, startling Brutus and the other men in the room. Brutus looked at me with surprise and then anger.

"Who the hell are you?" He demanded.

"I'm here because you fucked up a lot of people's lives," I replied, my voice steady.

Brutus sneered at me. "You think you can take me down? I have an army at my disposal."

"I don't need an army to take down a coward like you," I retorted.

Brutus' face turned red with rage. "You dare speak to me like that? I'll have you killed!"

"You won't be able to do anything once I'm done with you," I said, stepping closer to him.

Brutus tried to make a move toward me, but I quickly overpowered him. We engaged in a heated struggle, but my strength and determination were greater than his. I managed to overpower him and deliver the fatal blow.

As Brutus lay dying on the floor, he looked up at me with fear and confusion in his eyes. "Why?" He choked out.

His guests didn't bother doing anything. They couldn't see my face too thanks to the balaclava.

"Because you deserve it," I replied, my voice cold and devoid of emotion.

With Brutus dead, I quickly made my exit from the villa, making sure to avoid any other guards that might be patrolling the area. I made my way to the docks where the American CIA agents were waiting for me.

As I approached the boat, one of the agents greeted me. "You made it," he said coldly.

"Yeah, I did," I replied, feeling a sense of accomplishment wash over me.

The agents helped me onto the boat and we quickly set off toward the mainland. As we sailed away from the oasis, I couldn't help but feel a sense of sadness at leaving Oliver behind. But I knew that this was the only way I could ensure a future for both of us.

As we approached the mainland, the agents informed me that they would be taking me to a secure location where I would receive the treatment I needed. I nodded, feeling a sense of gratitude toward them.

I knew that the road ahead was going to be difficult, but I was ready to face whatever challenges came my way. With Oliver and our cub waiting for me, I had the strength and motivation to keep fighting.

CHAPTER 7

Oliver

My eyes fluttered open and I woke up. My arm and my hand looked for Bruno, but they found nothing. Panicked, I was startled and immediately sat up on the bed. My eyes were fully open now and I was scanning my surroundings.

Bruno was nowhere in my hotel room.

Maybe he is outside doing whatever.

That was a thought that crossed my mind, but I didn't believe it. I couldn't smell his scent. I couldn't feel his presence anywhere nearby. It was different for us shifters. We could feel people even if they were not too far away from us.

The fact that I couldn't feel his presence or smell his scent told me a lot.

My arms were already trembling. He couldn't have disappeared, right? He couldn't have ghosted me like some human 'friends' did to me in high school.

No, no way. He told me that I was his mate and that we were going to live together happily forever. That was what he told me and I knew he meant it. It couldn't be any different.

I got off the bed, slipping my feet into my shoes and putting on my clothes. He took me all the way from the campsite where we were to here and it was a nice gesture, but I didn't want to be thinking about that. I wanted to know where he was because my heart ached for him and missed him. My mind couldn't work well right now without him by my side.

And then, my eyes noticed a small note left on top of the nightstand. Could it be his? Part of me was hoping that it was and the other part was hoping that it wasn't.

I had seen this exact scene playing out in different movies and I knew how they all ended. They ended with the character finding out that his loved one left him. They might or might not reunite after that.

But I didn't want to be that character. I wanted my happy ending with Bruno and no price was too steep for that.

My hand was trembling, but I still picked up the note. I closed my eyes, even stopped breathing, and then I opened the note.

The handwriting was difficult to read, but I was able to make out the words.

Oliver... I'm so sorry that I'm doing this. I'm leaving. I'm going to America because the government is going to perform surgery on me. I have brain cancer.

I'm sorry I didn't tell you that. I didn't want to because I didn't want to worry you. You already probably have a lot on your mind, anyway.

But don't worry. They say that I'm going to be out for a few days. Maybe a couple of weeks. No more than that. After that, I'll seek you out. I'll go back to the oasis and I'll find you.

Don't worry about me. Just enjoy your days in that amazing place.

Tears were running down my cheeks. I couldn't believe it. He left me. I mean, it was for a good reason, but I didn't even know where to begin from.

He had brain cancer? He was fine when he was with me. No signs at all that he was ill. I knew that he was hiding something from me, but I didn't think that it was something as serious as brain cancer.

And it ached my heart because I didn't know if he was going to survive. I wasn't going to pretend that I knew a lot about modern-day medicine, but as far as I was aware, cancer was still a big complicated thing to cure, and it probably wasn't going to be any different for Bruno.

But now that I was thinking that he lied to me about something so important, could I even say that he didn't lie about his name too?

Could it be that his name was different?

I didn't know. There was nothing for me to cling to and think that he didn't lie about his name. And yet, something deep within my heart told me that he didn't lie about that.

But it would be smart. If he was working for the American government, it was smart that he didn't tell me his true name.

I didn't know what to think, shaking my head, closing my eyes, and crumpling the small note in my hand. I didn't hate Bruno, but I was disappointed, sad, and angry at everything.

I was angry at his fucking brain cancer because if it wasn't for it, he would be okay and we would be together.

I just didn't know what to do. My hand was roaming my belly, thinking about his baby. He left me with his baby. He told me that he was going to be back in a few days, but what if he never came back? What if he died during surgery?

There were so many possibilities. I couldn't even go after him. I didn't even know where he was, to be honest. He could be anywhere.

Plus, it wasn't like the CIA would let me get close to him anyway. They would put so many barriers between me and him that they would almost make me give up. But I would never.

I exhaled and inhaled several times.

My mother taught me that doing this could help me calm down in any given situation, but it was only a very weak solution. It wasn't helping that much.

So, okay. I decided to bring myself back to this moment and consider what I should do next. Bruno was going to have surgery, everything was going to be okay, and then he was going to be back right here and he was going to look for me in this room.

So, for a few days, I was going to extend my vacation here — because I would leave the oasis tomorrow otherwise, before reading his note — and then, when he was back, because of course he was going to be, I would slap him in his face so hard he would regret doing this to me, and then we would laugh about it over some drinks.

Yeah. That was what was going to happen.

I had someone who could help me through this, even if she couldn't know everything. That person was my mother.

I called her and she immediately picked up, "Hey, honey. It's been a while. How has it been in the oasis?"

"It's been great, mom. Better than I thought."

There was a moment of silence, her mind probably wondering what exactly I meant by that. "What happened?"

"I met my mate here in the oasis, Mom. I'm pregnant with his baby."

"Uhh, what? I didn't think that you were going to find your mate by accident there. But it's wonderful news, anyway. What's his name? What is he like?"

I bit my bottom lip. This was going to be complicated. It brought me so many feelings thinking about what Bruno was like.

"His name is Bruno, Mom, and he's amazing and you really have to meet him."

"Now, you're really making me excited about seeing him. You are coming back home tomorrow, right? I can meet him there with you."

I wasn't going to tell my mom about Bruno disappearing and leaving me with his baby. For now, it was better that she thought he was going to be with me when I came back home.

"You will meet him, Mom and you will have a great time with him. He is a really great guy. So, I'm extending my vacation. We are staying here together for a little while longer."

"Well, honey, if you are saying so, then he really must be."

There was a pause and she later asked, "And what are you going to do after finishing your degree? Are you going to look for work or will he provide for you both?"

"I don't know, mom. We haven't had the time to discuss it yet."

At least I didn't have to lie to my mom about that, I supposed.

"Darling, I'm delighted to learn that things are going well for you. I want to see you in person soon; it's been too long since we last saw each other."

Yeah. It'd been a while since I last saw my mom in person.

We talked a little bit more about ourselves, what I was going to do here in the oasis with Bruno — which made me sadder than I already was about him — and I told her that I would bring her a gift upon returning home.

CHAPTER 8

Bruno

My eyes slowly opened and all I could see were the bright, white walls surrounding me. I didn't remember arriving at this place. I remembered that I set up a deal with the CIA to operate on my brain cancer. This was the hospital they took me to. No doubt about it.

There was a person in the room. He must be one of the CIA agents. They must have told him that I was going to wake up at about now. He was looking out the window, not noticing yet that I woke up.

I tried to sit up, but my body was weak and I couldn't feel my legs fully yet. I could feel them somewhat, but I couldn't control them.

Apparently, the brain surgery was a success and my body was recovering slowly from it.

He noticed the noise I made and I noticed that he was someone I was familiar with. He was the one who approached me for the job. I never thought that I would work for the American government, much less for the fucking CIA.

Things were weird.

He stopped by my side, sitting on the hospital bed. "You're awake, Bruno. That's good."

"So, how was the surgery? A resounding success?"

He glanced down, seeming a little sad. "For the most part, yes. The doctors managed to remove the cancer from your brain and they don't think that it will come back in any form."

"Uhh, that's great. I can't wait to get out of here and go on with my life. Don't you forget that you told me you were going to pay me handsomely for the job."

He chuckled slightly, but there was nothing funny about it. "I didn't forget about that part of our agreement, Bruno, but there is something important you should know. The doctors told me that you were going to recover in a few days, but it's actually been... three years. You've been in a coma ever since the start of the surgery. The doctors couldn't do anything about it. Your brain just couldn't handle the surgery well."

My heart leaped. I couldn't believe it. It was already three years after that job I did for the CIA? My head was spinning.

I tried sitting up again, but my entire body hurt. He put his hand on my belly, saying, "Don't force yourself, Bruno. Your body is still recovering and even though I'm no doctor, I can tell that you're going to stay here for at least a few more weeks, and you're probably going to need some physical therapy sessions."

There was a small smile on his face, but again, this – all this – wasn't funny.

"It's been three fucking years, you bastard. I lost three fucking years of my life. How do you think I'm feeling about that?"

"You know what happened to me, Bruno. The CIA kept me in the dark for ten years when I was working for them. I even thought they'd forgotten about me. Those were ten years of my life that I lost as well."

I opened my mouth to rebuke him, but I knew he was right. He told me about that assignment he had been sent to. It had almost nearly destroyed his life.

"You're going to be fine, Bruno. Everything is going to be okay for you."

My head hurt, my hand on my forehead. "Shit. Is it worrying that I don't remember anything that happened in the oasis? I remember going there, but I don't remember anything after that."

He exhaled. "That is something the doctors were worried about. Partial amnesia. Your brain suffered a lot in the surgery and you probably lost your memories of what happened there."

My heart ached. For some reason, I could feel deep within my heart that something incredible happened in the oasis, but I couldn't remember exactly what it was. It couldn't be just that I had a great time surfing the waves and playing beach soccer.

No, that couldn't be everything.

He stood up, shuffling to the door, and I asked, "So, this is it? You're just going to leave me alone here?"

"I came here because we were doing that together, Bruno. It was a mutual assignment to get rid of Brutus. Everything worked to perfection as far as I'm concerned. Your body and your mind are weak right now, but you will heal."

I will be fine. Motherfucker. He doesn't understand anything about me.

And here I thought that he was my friend. He never was. *There are no friends in the CIA or the American government.*

Three fucking years. Lost three fucking years of my life working for the CIA. It will never happen again. They better give me my money and I'll retire.

I was, what, thirty-eight years old now? I was too old to find my mate. I guessed that it just wasn't supposed to happen to me.

For the following weeks, I did multiple therapies to get my body back to the shape that it was, including my mind. My brain was working fine, but I still couldn't remember what happened in the oasis and why there was a huge hole in my chest.

After those weeks, I was outside of the hospital, looking at the same man who brought me here. His dark sunglasses hid his eyes from me, but I knew that even though he posed a tough exterior, he was a man with feelings as well.

"This is it, Bruno. The money has already been delivered to your bank account and you don't owe us anything. Spend it however you like. The president is satisfied with your service to our country."

Yeah, more like their country, but whatever. We didn't ask for the

American government to come here. I didn't ask for the American government to reach out to me.

"Whatever we had, it's over. I hope I will never see you again," I barked.

He didn't say anything. There was a taxi behind him waiting for me. I opened the door, sat inside, and the taxi began to drive. I assumed that it was taking me home.

It should still be mine, but most likely it was infested with cockroaches and all kinds of other nasty insects. Not to mention the thick layer of dust everywhere. *Don't think the CIA cleaned up my house for me, after all.*

The taxi pulled away and I found myself looking outside, admiring the buildings, the people, the nature, and everything else. I was trying to cling to something, anything, and I was trying to find a new meaning to my life.

I was leaving behind my old life as a merc and an assassin. I was going to retire and that was it. But what was I going to do in my retirement? Was I going to the oasis again in the hopes of finding out what happened there?

The hole in my chest remained and no matter what I did, I didn't feel like I could fill it with something.

Even the driver appeared to notice something was wrong with me. He asked, looking at me from the rearview mirror, "Everything okay with you, sir?"

I didn't know what to say. Part of me hoped that he really cared about me, but I figured he was just trying to make some small conversation with me and nothing more than that.

"Everything is okay with me. What about you?" I lied.

A small smile formed on his face. "Everything's fine with me; thank you for asking. My wife is expecting to deliver our next child next week, and she is scheduled to have a C-section."

His wife was pregnant. I didn't know why, but the moment he said that, I began to wonder if what happened to me in the oasis was related to pregnancy somehow. But, that was crazy.

I couldn't have gotten myself involved with an Omega, right? No, I didn't think so. Even though I probably found the oasis a great place, I couldn't have fallen in love with anyone, or gotten that person pregnant.

I shook my head, a smile on my face. What a stupid idea that was.

I returned my attention to the taxi driver and said, "Good luck to you and her. I hope that you two have a good life together."

"Thank you, sir."

He continued to talk about his life and I pretended that I was listening. I wasn't really interested in his life. It was better than mine and my life was changed drastically from one moment to the other, even though it was years since I entered the surgery room.

But after signing into my bank account and checking the sum that was there, I couldn't help but feel that there might be hope for me in the future. Even though my life as a merc had been adventurous, it didn't make me filthy rich just like I was now.

In the coming days, after mentally recovering from all of this, I planned to search for a nice house to buy. I had always dreamed of owning a house with a beautiful pool, so it would be a spacious one with a massive pool for me to enjoy and host parties.

But, a funny thing about the pool. It kind of made me remember something about water, but even though it was right at the tip of my tongue, I couldn't say exactly what it was.

CHAPTER 9

Bruno

I adjusted my tie, entering the house with the real estate agent who was trying everything in her power to sell it to me. She was a stunning woman with fiery red hair cascading down her shoulders and all the way to the top of her ass.

Her hips swayed gently as she proceeded "As you can see, this is the living room. It's fully furnished, but you can ask us to remove everything so you can decorate it to your liking."

The house was nice; a mixture of old and new with huge windows letting the sunlight through. This was what I imagined my house was going to be like when I was growing up. I never thought that one day I would have enough money to make that dream come true.

"I'm still thinking about that," I said.

She winked at me. "No worries, Mr. Stormpelt. Take your time."

Oh, I'm definitely going to take my time with this.

Time for me to indulge myself a little. Hadn't had the opportunity to do that in my former life as a merc.

She continued, moving to the windows facing the outside garden. She pointed at it with her hand. "This is the front garden. As you can see, it's already finished and the plants are all grown, but you can change that too however you want. Just be sure to tell me."

"I'll definitely tell you if I want that."

She proceeded, this time going to the kitchen. The kitchen itself was bigger than my previous house. I couldn't stay there for long. Even though I owned it, it was... It brought me memories that I didn't want to remember.

Not to mention that it was too old and it was infested with cockroaches and other insects, just as I'd thought.

"Mr. Stormpelt, this is the kitchen. It has everything you may need. Just like the living room, it's fully furnished and everything has been cleaned for you. However, in case you find that there is something that is not to your liking, just be sure to inform me."

This time, I didn't say anything. There was no need to, not to mention that I was wondering what the bedroom really looked like. It was one thing to have seen it in the photos on the company's website, and it was probably going to be a different thing to see it in person.

"All right, Mr. Stormpelt. Let's go upstairs."

Mr. Stormpelt. It wasn't the first time that someone was calling me that way instead of using my first name, but it was always weird and I didn't think that I would ever get used to it.

She continued up the stairs and the moment that I put my foot on the first step, I heard someone quickly entering the living room from behind me. Turning around just as quickly, my eyes found a sweet and cute guy who immediately stopped just as he saw me. His face went pale. It was as if he was seeing a ghost or someone was pointing a gun to his face and he was going to die right here and now.

But that couldn't be the case. Maybe he was just socially awkward and he didn't think that there were going to be so many people in my future house, even though it was just the three of us.

The real estate agent whose name I didn't care about immediately noticed what was happening and she turned around on her heels.

"Oliver, what are you doing? I thought that you were going to come only in about thirty minutes from now. I'm still not done showing the house to Mr. Stormpelt."

His face was still pale. I felt sorry for the guy, but I couldn't do anything about it.

He mumbled something. He really was socially awkward and very unsure of himself. I was too old to find a mate, but if I were younger, I was pretty sure that he would be the one.

Or that he might be one of the possible ones. I didn't know much about shifter dating anymore. It was as if I lost touch with that during the time that I was in a coma.

The ginger woman proceeded to Oliver with determined steps. She whirled him around and pushed him away from me. "Oliver, come on, get a hold of yourself. You are ruining this. I'm trying to sell the house to my customer, and this is important to me."

Sheesh, woman. You don't need to worry so much about that. Of course I'm going to buy this house and you're going to get your big, fat bonus.

During the next few minutes, she continued to show me the house and, eventually, I stepped outside. The last thing I thought I was going to see was the same omega from before. Though he'd already left.

And I knew that he was an omega because of his scent. It was different from that of a normal human, or an alpha.

The ginger turned to me, asking, "So, everything to your liking, Mr. Stormpelt?"

"Absolutely. Think that I'm going to buy this house."

She gave me a smile of approval, showing how happy she was with my decision, even though there was nothing to decide, to begin with.

She turned her attention to Oliver. That was his name, wasn't it? I heard her saying it.

"Come on, Oliver. I need to go to the agency to finish this deal."

He wrung his hands. "There's actually something that I need to do for our client, as you should remember."

She squinted her eyes. "I hope that it's not what I think it is."

And what are you thinking it is? That he is going to steal your bonus? Come on, that's ridiculous. There is no way a sweet omega like Oliver here can ever even think about doing something like that.

"It's not," he reassured her.

"Well, see you later, Oliver." She turned her attention to me, smiling widely. "And I hope to see you again as well, Mr. Stormpelt."

I waved my hand. "Sure, I'm sure we will."

And with that said, she went to her car and drove away. Oliver had something to do for me, and I was somewhat curious about it. What could it be?

And for a moment, there was only silence. He wasn't even looking at me. He wasn't even looking anywhere in particular. *Maybe he is thinking about something worrying in his life.*

That was what I told myself, anyway. As for me, I was waiting for my things to be delivered to this house so that I could begin the move-in process today. I didn't want to sleep in my old house anymore.

Eventually, I exhaled and asked, "What do you want to do for me, kiddo?"

"Bruno, what happened?" He asked sheepishly.

I arched my right eyebrow. "What happened with what?"

He turned to me, his eyes teary. Shit. Was he going to cry? I wasn't in the mood to deal with that. Not to mention that I didn't want anything sad marring my day. It was being good for me.

"What happened between us? You disappeared. You told me that you were going to be back to the oasis in a few days, but it's been three years and I found you by accident."

Shit. This guy knew me from the oasis?

"Wait, what's happening here? You know me?"

He grabbed my arms, shaking me. His voice trembled as he said as loudly as he could, "Bruno, stop playing with me! You left me! You ghosted me! You left me with your child and you told me that I was your forever mate."

I shook my body free, immediately barking, "Let go of me, kiddo. If I know you from that place, I don't remember anything."

"You don't... remember anything? How?"

Shit. I put my hand on my forehead, shaking my head. "Look, kiddo, I was in a coma for three years and I lost some of my memories. If I met you in the oasis, it doesn't mean anything to me anymore." I took a deep breath, calming myself down. "But you said that I have a child? You're not doing this to skim money from me, are you?"

He shook his head immediately. "No, I'm not. I'm actually doing okay for myself, making more money than I know what to do with."

There was a pause and he continued, "You told me that you had brain cancer. Here, I even kept the note you left for me. I've been carrying it with me closely this entire time because I've been holding onto the hope you were going to come back to me eventually." He chuckled. "Huh. Didn't think that it was going to be me accidentally finding you."

He handed me the note, his hand was trembling, and even though I didn't remember ever writing those words, there was no denying that it was my handwriting and that it said exactly what he told me it said.

Plus, not many people knew about my surgery.

He had to be someone I met in the oasis. Question was: just how much did we get to know each other?

CHAPTER 10

Oliver

He crumpled the note in his hand, throwing it away. "So, you know me."

"Of course I know you, Bruno. When we were in the oasis, you meant everything to me."

My eyes were teary. I was doing everything possible not to cry right now.

He exhaled, putting his hand on the doorway. "Doesn't mean anything to me because I don't remember you, Oliver, but you are sweet and I like you."

I stepped forward, wishing to grab his hand, wishing to do anything, but I couldn't.

"You don't feel anything for me? You don't feel what you felt when you found me for the first time? You told me that we shifters always feel something uncontrollable and strong when we meet our mate for the first time."

He exhaled again, looking away. "And here I thought that today was going to be an uneventful day. I thought that today I was going to be focusing on what this house should look like so it makes me feel like the happiest bear in the world."

I blinked a few times. "I don't understand, Bruno."

He turned, facing the interior of his house. Gesturing with his hand, he said, "Come with me. Let's talk about this inside."

I didn't think doing that was going to make any difference, but I was going to do it anyway.

We entered the living room. His house was nice — nicer than mine was, to be honest. Even though I was doing well for myself - enough to keep myself and our baby fed - it was not enough to buy a place such as this one.

"I don't remember anything about shifter dating, Oliver. I was thirty-five years old when I met you. That was the end of my - shit, I don't even know how to call it. Before we get too old, we can feel something strong for each other, but after a certain age, we don't feel the same thing anymore."

"I didn't know that, Bruno. I actually don't know anything about shifter dating. You seemed to know so much. I was learning so much from you."

"Here, come with me to the bar room. I'm going to pour you a drink. Maybe it's going to help us get through this and help me figure out what to do."

As we entered the bar room, I asked him "So, you know that I'm not telling you a lie, right? You know that something strong happened between us, don't you?"

He looked at me, a sly smile on his face. "I'm not going to say that. Let's drink, think about what's happening here, and then we can decide what to do."

He handed me the drink. Whiskey on rocks. Couldn't be any better than this, to be honest. I really was going to need something strong to get the edge off, feel less emotional about this.

"After three years, I didn't think I would ever see you."

"I'm sorry about what happened, Oliver. I went to the surgery room expecting to wake up in a few days, but the doctors couldn't anticipate that I was going to be in a coma."

I took a long gulp of the whiskey. It was warm and made me feel better about what was happening already, but it was far from enough. I actually didn't think that there was anything capable of making me feel normal ever again in my life.

"So, what really happened? You should've told me you had brain cancer. I would have understood. I would have been by your side at the hospital the entire time until you woke up."

He poured himself a drink, taking a sip of it. "It wouldn't have worked that way, Oliver. Shit." He put his hand on his forehead, shaking his head. "I don't even know if I should tell you the whole truth. I fear for your life."

"You fear for my life? What do you mean?"

"I was a dangerous person three years ago. Still am, but I'm not doing the same thing I was. Have more than enough money to do whatever I want now, all because of a fucking job in the oasis."

I took a step backward. His words were beginning to instill fear in me. "What do you mean, Bruno? What exactly did you do? I asked you back then what you did for a living and you evaded my question every time."

He chuckled, sipping his drink again. "I was smart doing that. Was smart to keep you in the dark."

I hurled the glass away and it shattered on the wall. Bruno didn't even blink.

He exhaled, looking at the liquid and the glass shards on the floor. "Do you really want to know everything? I think it might change your opinion about me."

I stepped forward, my hands gripping the bar table. "Of course I want to know everything, Bruno! You are my mate! You are the father of my child!"

He put down his drink and looked at the ceiling. "All right, Oliver. I'm going to tell you everything and you are going to hate me so much."

And he began to explain everything, detail by detail, day by day, month by month, year by year. His life as a mercenary was hectic and he did a lot of wrong things. He wasn't the nice alpha I thought he was.

Before me was a different man. He was not the same person I thought he was.

He took a long gulp of his drink. He chuckled and said, "See? I told you that you were going to hate me."

"Yeah, you're right, but only partially. I should hate you, but I don't."

His eyes widened. "Why not? You have every reason to hate me."

"I do, but it feels like you were forced into that life. It wasn't your choice."

He held my gaze, trying to think about what to say next.

He went around the bar table, proceeding to me. "I've told you everything about my life. You know the kind of person that you are dealing with. I shouldn't be your mate."

"And yet, you are."

He remained before me, breathing slowly. I put my hand on his chest, feeling his heart beating. "Do you know something we can do to change everything for the better?" I asked.

He cleared his throat and responded, "No, I don't, Oliver."

This," I said before cupping his cheeks and getting on my tiptoes to kiss him. He allowed me, our lips connecting. It was a passionate kiss right from the start. It was telling me so much.

It was telling me that he was capable of feeling what he felt for me back then in the oasis.

His lips were wet and warm, just like I remembered them. It was as if there was no time skip between us. It was as if we had always been together and this was just another day for us where we expressed our love.

He put his arm around me, pulling me closer. I could feel his chest pressed against mine. Once again, I could feel his heart beating. I could feel how warm he was.

Bruno pulled his head back slightly and said, "Gosh, I missed this so much."

Was he referring to kissing me or just kissing people in general? I didn't know, but I was engrossed in our kiss and I wasn't thinking about anything else. I was only thinking about our kiss and how good it was.

I could feel his tongue going inside my mouth, and from that moment, he was the only one dictating how we should proceed with kissing each other. He was relentless, just like I remembered he was.

It was good and I was getting aroused by the minute. It felt like we were already kissing for several minutes nonstop.

"I think I may be remembering some things," he whispered into my ear, making my heart race. Could it be? Could it be that the simple act of kissing him was bringing back his memories? I didn't know, but it was the only thing I could cling to, so I was doubling down on it, and it was everything I thought it was going to be.

I had longed for this moment for what felt like an eternity, and now, maybe it was time to finally put my life back on track in terms of relationships. After all, after Bruno not coming back from his operation, I didn't date anyone.

How could I? I had his child with me and it would be wrong if I dated someone while still thinking about my true mate.

CHAPTER 11

Oliver

Bruno's hands were now all over me, and I could feel the heat radiating off of his body. He was just as aroused as I was, and it was clear that he wanted more. He pulled me closer, his hands roaming down my back and settling on my hips. I could feel his hardness pressing against me, and it sent a shiver down my spine.

It was just like in the oasis.

Without breaking our kiss, Bruno began to undress me. He started with my shirt, pulling it over my head and tossing it aside. His hands then moved to my pants, undoing the button and zipper with ease. I could feel his fingers tracing the waistband of my underwear, and I knew that he was teasing me. He wanted me to beg for it.

But I wasn't going to give in that easily. I wanted to make this moment last as long as possible. I reached up and began to undo the buttons on Bruno's shirt, revealing his toned chest and abs. I could feel his muscles tensing beneath my fingers, and it only made me want him more.

I removed his tie too, tossing it aside.

We continued to undress each other hurriedly, our hands fumbling in our desperation to feel each other's skin. Bruno's pants were next, and I couldn't help but admire the way his boxers hugged his hips. He kicked off his shoes and socks, and I did the same, our clothes forming a pile on the floor.

We were now both standing in nothing but our underwear, and I could feel the tension between us growing. Bruno's eyes were dark with desire, and I knew that he wanted me just as much as I wanted him. He reached out and pulled me toward him, our bodies pressed against each other once again.

"So, we did this in the oasis?" He asked.

I nodded and confirmed, "We did, and a lot more, too."

I could feel his hardness pressed against my stomach, and I knew that he was aching to come. I reached down and began to stroke him through his boxers, and he let out a low groan. He was so hard, and I could feel him throbbing in my hand.

Bruno then reached down and hooked his fingers into the waistband of my underwear, pulling them down. I stepped out of them, now completely naked before him. He took a moment to admire my body, his eyes traveling up and down my torso.

I could feel myself growing harder under his gaze, and I knew that I couldn't wait any longer. I reached down and hooked my fingers into the waistband of his boxers, pulling them down. He stepped out of them, and we were both now completely naked before each other.

The air between us was electric, and I knew that we couldn't wait any longer. Bruno pulled me toward him, our lips meeting once again in a passionate kiss. His hands were roaming all over my body, and I could feel myself growing more and more aroused by the second.

I reached down and wrapped my hand around his hardness, stroking him slowly. He let out a low groan, and I knew that he was enjoying it. He reached down and began to stroke me as well, and I could feel myself getting closer and closer to the edge.

We continued to pleasure each other, our bodies moving in sync. I could feel myself getting closer and closer to the edge, and I knew that I couldn't hold on much longer. Bruno must have sensed it as well, as he picked me up and carried me over to the couch.

He laid me down gently, his body hovering over mine. I could feel his hardness pressing against me, and I knew that I wanted him inside of me. He reached over to the side table and grabbed a condom, quickly putting it on.

He then positioned himself at my entrance, and I could feel myself tensing up in anticipation. He pushed inside of me slowly, and I let out a low moan. It felt amazing, and I never wanted it to end.

We began to move together, our bodies in perfect harmony. I could feel myself getting closer and closer to the edge, and I knew that I couldn't hold on much longer. Bruno must have sensed it as well, as he began to thrust harder and faster.

I could feel myself getting closer and closer to the edge, and finally, I reached my peak. I let out a loud moan as I came, my body shaking with pleasure. Bruno followed shortly after, his body tensing up as he reached his own climax.

We lay there for a moment, our bodies entwined and our breathing heavy. I could feel Bruno's heartbeat racing against my chest, and I knew that we had just shared something truly special.

As we lay there, I couldn't help but think about the future. I knew that Bruno still didn't remember everything, but I was hopeful that one day, he would. And when that day came, I knew that we would be able to pick up right where we left off.

For now, though, I was just happy to be in his arms, feeling his warmth and his love. I knew that we still had a long road ahead of us, but I was ready to face it with Bruno by my side.

He chuckled, kissing the top of my head. "You really are something else, Oliver. I thought that you were just a sweet Omega, but you are really so much more than that. No wonder I probably fell in love with you back in the oasis."

I looked at his eyes. "We did. We did so much more than that. You promised me that we would be together for the rest of our lives because that is our destiny."

He looked at the ceiling, seeming pensive. "Destiny. I don't know what that word means anymore."

I placed my hands on his chest, stroking it. "You're going to remember it, Bruno. I know you can because you are strong and determined."

His eyes locked with mine again. "You know everything I did and yet you don't hate me and feel scared of me."

I shook my head. "I don't, Bruno. I feel that you really are my mate."

There was a moment of silence and I chuckled after remembering something funny. "You looked so different all dressed in the suit and the tie before," I said.

He turned to see me, arching his right eyebrow. "What do you mean, Oliver?"

I exhaled, remembering that very eventful day in the oasis. "When you were there with me, you were completely naked. Even when you were walking around other people, you didn't bother to put on clothes."

His eyes widened. "Seriously?"

I nodded, a small smile on my face. "Yes, seriously. Everybody was looking at you with wide eyes and you still didn't bother to put on clothes."

"It kind of feels like the surgery did more than just remove the brain cancer and some of my memories. Feels like it changed my personality as well."

I caressed his cheek, feeling how warm it was. "I know, Bruno, but if you accept spending more time with me, getting to know me again, maybe you will remember to be your former self again."

"Yeah, maybe I will," he said and proceeded not to say anything. For the next few minutes, we didn't say anything. We just stared at nothing in particular, thinking about everything that happened.

"So, what did you do after realizing that I wasn't going to come back?" He asked.

"I was frustrated, angry, and I cried a lot. I didn't know what to tell my mother because I told her that I met you and that you were amazing. She probably still hates you because she thinks you abandoned me."

He chuckled. "That's something I'll need to address. I'll need to talk to her and explain everything that happened. If she is as open-minded as you are, she will understand what happened, especially as long as you are by my side to help me."

I grabbed his hand, squeezing it. "I'm going to be there. I'm going to take you to see my mom and especially our child. You may be thinking that it's not really your son, but once you see him, you will realize that it is indeed yours."

He kissed my cheek. "I know, Oliver. Tomorrow morning, the first thing we are going to do is to see those amazing people. If they are with you, then I know that they have good hearts."

CHAPTER 12

Bruno

After the delivery company delivered my things to my new house, I began to unpack everything and put it all in the right places. It took a lot of time, but still, less time than it would have taken if I were alone. Oliver helped me. He didn't have to, but he still did.

It was yet another reason for me to think that he was indeed my fated mate. I *may* be feeling something akin to that, even though I didn't know for sure.

We slept together as well. The sex we had was amazing and I would never forget it. It also made me remember — kind of — what happened in the oasis. Maybe Oliver was the key to bringing my memories back.

But again, I didn't know that for sure. Better not to nurture false hope about anything.

He woke up by my side, a smile on his face. "Good morning," I said. This was good. I could imagine myself waking up every morning with Oliver by my side. And, chuckling to myself, I couldn't help but wonder what the real estate agent from before would think after finding out that we were dating, me and Oliver.

"Good morning," he said as well.

I sat up on the bed, putting my feet on the floor. Turning to see him, I said, "I'm not a great cook, Oliver, and I want you to have an excellent meal this morning. I say we go to a nice restaurant before you take me to see your mother and my child."

"His name is Adrian, just so you know. He looks just like you."

I smiled. "Looks just like me, you say? Now, you've made me even more interested in seeing him for the first time."

He grabbed my hand, squeezing it. "You are."

I got off the bed, standing up. "Time to take a shower and get dressed. It's going to be a long day, especially if your mother still hates me so much."

He went to me, hugging me tightly and chuckling as well. "Don't worry about my mother. Even if she makes a scene because of you suddenly appearing, she'll come around."

I ruffled his hair. "I trust you, Oliver. It really is beginning to feel like I didn't even lose my memories."

His eyes welled up with tears. "Are you sure? Is everything really coming back to you?"

I shook my head, erasing any possibility of making him feel false hope. "No, not really, but I trust you, Oliver, and that is more than good enough for me."

He bit his bottom lip, seeming disappointed.

I grabbed his hand, squeezing it to reassure him. "Come on Oliver. Let's take a shower together and then find a good place for breakfast."

He perked up, seeming happier now. "Okay, Bruno! That's exactly what I was thinking we should do."

So, we took a shower together. It was lovingly erotic and we even had sex in the shower box. We spent more time showering together than we should, but it was okay. It was just another way for us to continue to bond together.

It really was beginning to feel like he was my fated mate.

After finishing showering together, we went to a restaurant downtown. The place was cozy and small, but the food was delicious. We ate as much as possible, but not without losing track of time. I didn't want to arrive at his place, where his mother was also living, too late.

After that, I drove to his place. My vehicle was a sleek SUV with more than enough space for both of us, including Adrian. And thinking about my child, I couldn't help but wonder if he really looked just like me.

That would confirm that he was my child and I would take him to live with me. *Live with us,* to be more precise. Oliver was going to move in with me.

We arrived at his place. He got out of my SUV, proceeded to open the door to his house, and his mother immediately appeared, opening her arms out wide and hugging her son.

"Oliver! I was worried about you. You didn't come home last night. You told me that you were going to come. I took care of Adrian in your absence, so you don't need to worry about him. He was a little fussy without you, though."

Oliver smiled. "I know, Mom, and there is someone I want you to meet."

I got out of my SUV slowly and carefully. I was nervous because I knew how his mom was going to react. First time in a long time that I was nervous about something. It was three years since the beginning of the surgery, after all.

I waved my hand and before Oliver could say anything, I decided to be the one to introduce myself. After stepping forward, I said, "Mrs. Wolfson, I'm Bruno. Oliver must have talked about me with you."

Her eyes widened immediately and she rushed toward me, slamming her finger on my chest. "How dare you come here? You left my son! You left him with a child! How dare you come back?"

Oliver immediately with himself between me and his mom. He pushed her away from me slightly, pleading, "Mom, calm down. Hear me out. It wasn't his fault. He left the island because he had brain cancer that he needed to operate. He was in a coma for the last three years and he lost his memories. Honestly, it's a miracle that he decided to continue from where we stopped. He came here to see you, ask for your forgiveness, and to see our son as well."

She looked at Oliver, her body still shaking in anger. "Oliver, are you really sure about that? What if he leaves you again?"

"I would never do that, Mrs. Wolfson. I may not remember everything that happened between me and Oliver in the oasis, but I remember that he was someone special to me. The hole in my chest is beginning to be filled up by him."

She started to calm down a little, but it wasn't sufficient.

"Oliver, I'm still not sure about this. You cried a lot when you told me that he wasn't going to come. And you didn't tell me that he had brain cancer."

His eyes were teary when he said, "I know, Mom. I didn't tell you because I didn't want to anger you any more than you already were. I was just trying to do what I thought was best, but it appears that I made a big mistake."

"It was more than a mistake, Oliver. It was inconsiderate. You should have thought about how I would feel after finding out that you lied to me, and you knew that I was going to find out the truth one way or another eventually."

He looked down, stepping away from his mother.

"I need a cup of tea, or maybe two," she said before whirling around and striding inside Oliver's house. Meanwhile, Oliver's shoulders were hunched down.

I shuffled over to him, putting a hand on his shoulder. "For what it's worth, I think that went better than I thought."

"I'm so sorry about the way she treated you, Bruno. I should have thought that she was going to lash out at you."

I chuckled slightly. "Oliver, don't worry about that. I went through so much worse." I paused, remembering someone important. "Show me Adrian. I want to see him."

My son was probably around two years old now.

Oliver perked up, seeming happier now. "Let's go inside, then. He must be in his room playing with his toys."

We entered the house. Mrs. Wolfson was in the kitchen, preparing tea just as she said was going to be. I knew that she wasn't going to offer me a cup.

Oliver took me to one of the rooms in the house and he opened the door. Sitting on the floor and playing with a small toy car was a beautiful baby boy with brown hair and brown eyes.

Oliver didn't lie when he said that he looked just like me. Even the face itself was very familiar to mine. And yet, at the same time, he also took after Oliver. He was an omega just like his father and just as cute.

I knelt on one knee, smiling, and said, "Hey, little guy. Everything okay with you?"

Oliver came to my side, kneeling as well. "Hey, Adrian. This is Bruno. He's a friend of mine and my partner. We are going to be living together."

I didn't know how much Adrian understood of what was happening. After all, he was only two years old. He was probably thinking that I was just one of Oliver's friends.

Either way, it was great that the family was finally reunited.

BRUNO'S EPILOGUE

3 years later...

Adrian climbed up on my lap, snuggling up to me. He whispered into my ear, "Daddy, I love you so much."

I ruffled his hair, saying, "I love you too, little guy."

Adrian was five years old now and understood that I was his father as much as Oliver was. It was difficult to tell him that without telling him everything. After all, I didn't want my son to find out that I was a merc who killed people for money.

I didn't want him to find out that the reason for my disappearance for three years was because I was working for the CIA in a very secretive operation.

He didn't need to know about those things. At least, not for now. Eventually, he might find out the truth on his own, but by then, I was hoping it wouldn't matter.

Nothing I could do about that. So much so that, at the moment, I was just enjoying this moment we were spending together.

This house was different to him when he came here. He was kind of lost in it because it was so big but began to get used to it after the first few weeks.

He had a lot of places here to play with his toys, so it was easy for him to get used to this new place.

He looked at me and I smiled, saying, "Okay, little guy, tell me what you want."

Every time that he said that he loved me, it was because he wanted something from me. He was old enough now to begin to learn to play video games, so sometimes he needed my credit card to buy something for his games. I wasn't a fan of microtransactions, but to indulge my son, I would do pretty much anything.

"Can I please have the new Apple Vision Pro that just came out? All my friends have it and I'm the only one feeling left out."

Apple Vision Pro? It was the first time I was hearing about it. I wasn't really the kind of guy to stay in the loop about new technologies.

"What is it, Adrian?"

He gestured with his hands, moving them from the front of his face and finishing the movement at the back of his head. "It's a virtual reality device, Dad. You've never heard about that? What about the Meta Quest 3?"

I shook my head. "No, little guy. I haven't heard a peep about those devices."

He pouted.

Maybe I was falling behind the times, but I didn't care. The only thing I cared about was that I had a good family with me and had enough money to provide for them without having to work ever again in my life.

I put my hand under his chin, lifting his head. "Cheer up, Adrian. I'm going to buy you the Vision Pro right now."

He perked up, his eyes gleaming with delight. "Really, daddy? That's amazing! I can't wait to show it to my friends at school."

He jumped off my lap, and we headed to the garage. I opened the door for him, he took a seat in the passenger seat, and I secured the safety belt around him. Afterward, I settled into the driver's seat.

Oliver came up to me suddenly, asking, "Where are you two going right now?"

"Adrian wants the new Apple Vision Pro, or whatever it's called. I don't know anything about it other than that apparently it's a virtual reality device."

His eyes widened knowingly. "Oh, I know about that device. I was thinking about getting one for myself too. It just might be useful for my work."

I kissed his cheek and said, "Leave it to me, then, honey. I'm going to the Apple Store by the mall and I'm going to buy two."

As we drove to the store, Adrian was bouncing with excitement in his seat. He couldn't wait to get his hands on the new virtual reality device and start exploring all the different games and experiences it had to offer.

When we arrived at the mall, I parked the car and helped Adrian out of his seat. He took my hand and we walked toward the Apple Store, his eyes fixed on the gleaming glass doors.

As soon as we stepped inside, a sales associate greeted us with a friendly smile. "Welcome to the Apple Store! How can I help you today?"

"We're looking for the new Apple Vision Pro," I said. "Do you have any in stock?"

The sales associate tapped on his iPad and nodded. "Yes, we do. It just came out today and we've had a lot of people coming in to buy it. Would you like to try it out before you make your purchase?"

"That would be great," I said, and Adrian nodded eagerly.

The sales associate led us over to a display area where we could try out the Vision Pro. He handed us each a pair of the goggles and showed us how to put them on.

As soon as I put on the goggles, I was transported to a virtual world. It was incredibly realistic and immersive, and I could see why Adrian was so excited about it. I tried out a few different games and experiences, and was impressed by the smooth and responsive controls.

After trying it out for a few minutes, I knew that we had to buy it. Adrian was already hooked, and I could tell that he was going to have hours of fun with it.

We bought three Vision Pros, actually, along with a few accessories, and then headed back home. Oliver was eager to try it out as well again, and the three of us spent the rest of the afternoon exploring different virtual worlds and playing games together.

As I watched Adrian and Oliver laughing and having fun, I felt a sense of contentment wash over me. It was moments like these that made all the hard work and sacrifices worth it. I was grateful to have a loving family and a home to come back to, and I knew that I would do whatever it took to protect them.

OLIVER'S EPILOGUE

1 year later...

"Man, I'm going to look so weird dressed like this," I said, checking my reflection in the mirror. Today was my marriage day. Today was the day I was going to get married to Bruno, something I thought would never happen after his disappearance.

But that happened years ago and it was just a wound in my chest that had long healed.

One of the people helping me get in my suit said, "Don't worry, Oliver. I'm sure that you're going to look great when you are stepping down the aisle."

I closed my eyes, imagining that moment. My heart was beating in excitement. I was thinking about how great it was going to be walking down the aisle to my mate.

We were going to have a normal human wedding. We thought about doing a shifter wedding, but we both knew that we weren't more shifter-like anymore. Both Bruno and I were living more with humans than with shifters, so we knew that this marriage was the perfect one for us.

Not to mention that Adrian was going to be watching everything, so I knew that he was more accustomed to human weddings than shifter weddings.

Could they even be called weddings too? Did they have weddings? Maybe I should look that up one day.

Also, maybe one day we would take Adrian to the shifter lands. We could also take him to the Oasis for Bears, where I met his father.

But thinking about the oasis, I couldn't help but feel a sudden surge of sadness in my heart. Even after all these years, Bruno couldn't remember what we experienced on those islands.

I shook my head, dismissing those thoughts. I didn't want to feel sad about anything at the moment.

The guy helping me with my suit finished adjusting my tie, smiling broadly. "All good, Oliver. You're good to go."

I smiled and looked at him. "Thank you. I don't know what I would be doing right now without you. I'm so clumsy when it comes to these kinds of things."

He opened a wide smile. "No problem, Oliver. You can come to me anytime you need help with pretty much anything I know."

I left his studio and proceeded to the limousine waiting for me. I chuckled, thinking about something funny. I insisted that Bruno didn't have to make me go there on a limousine, but he was more persistent about that than I was. In the end, I budged.

I entered the limousine, took a seat, and strapped the safety belt around me. As we drove toward the venue, I watched the buildings appear and disappear outside.

We weren't religious like some other humans were, so it was not a church. But the place was still beautiful. It was cozy and somewhat familiar.

I arrived there and someone opened the door for me. Again, I insisted that I didn't need someone opening and closing the door of the limousine for me, but Bruno was persistent about that too.

He told me that today was all about me and that I should be happy.

I was happy. I just didn't need to be pampered so much and people treating me like I was royalty.

My mother came to my side, interlinking her arm with mine. My father was absent in my life, so it had to be her the one to take me to my soon-to-be husband.

It took her almost forever to come around and become friends with Bruno, but in the end, everything worked out. They were more friends now than I thought they could ever be.

The two even shared a common hobby: tennis. Occasionally, they would go to one of the tennis courts in the city to play a few rounds and catch up on what was happening in their lives.

I took a deep breath and my mother reassured me, "Everything's going to be fine, honey. Bruno is waiting for you."

I knew that he was.

We started to walk down the aisle and everybody stood up, clapping and cheering at me, at us. I reached the spot where Bruno was waiting for me and my mother delivered me to him.

She winked at him and then sat on a bench, putting one leg on top of the other and folding her arms over her chest.

It was time to start the marriage.

As the officiant began the ceremony, I couldn't help but feel a flutter of nerves in my stomach. But when I looked over at Bruno, standing next to me, I felt a sense of calm wash over me. The officiant welcomed everyone and expressed their happiness for us, and I couldn't help but smile.

We exchanged vows, promising to love and cherish each other for the rest of our lives. As I spoke my vows, I could feel tears welling up in my eyes. I had never felt so sure of anything in my life. Bruno's vows were equally heartfelt, and I could see that he was just as emotional as I was.

After the vows, we exchanged rings, symbolizing our commitment to each other. The officiant pronounced us husband and husband, and the guests erupted into cheers and applause. Bruno and I shared our first kiss as a married couple, and then made our way back down the aisle, hand in hand. We were greeted with hugs and congratulations from our friends and family.

The reception was held in a nearby hall, and it was a joyous occasion. There was music, dancing, and plenty of food and drink. Bruno and I danced our first dance together as a married couple, and then invited everyone else to join us on the dance floor.

As the night went on, I couldn't help but feel grateful for everything that had led me to this moment. I was married to the man I loved, surrounded by the people who mattered most to me. It was a perfect ending to our love story.

End of Book 6

This series will continue in book 7! While I'm still writing it, you should check the previous entries:

1. Cautious Omega
2. Devoted Omega
3. Hesitant Omega
4. Conflicted Omega
5. Fleeing Omega

Don't forget to leave your review. It really helps me!

SIMILAR BOOKS

SERIES - BEARLY MATED DATING AGENCY

1. Omega's Grumpy Bear Shifter
2. Omega's Stubborn Bear Shifter
3. Omega's Cocky Bear Shifter
4. Omega's Possessive Bear Shifter
5. Omega's Obsessed Bear Shifter

SERIES - OMEGAVERSE MC

Bikers who stop at nothing to claim their Omega mates.

1. Omega for Obsessive Alpha
2. Omega for Protective Alpha
3. Omega for Jealous Alpha

SERIES - ALPHA MC

Bikers obsessed with knotting.

1. Omega's Possessive Alpha
2. Alpha's Surrogate Omega
3. Alpha's Shy Omega

SERIES - PREGNANT FOR HIM

Short, steamy, and always fertile.

1. Controlled by the Alpha 1: An MPREG Omegaverse Story
2. Controlled by the Alpha 2: An MPREG Omegaverse Story
3. Controlled by the Alpha 3: Dominating the Fertile Omega

ABOUT THE AUTHOR

Steamy MM stories, baby! Michael Levi can't go a day without sitting down and putting into words all the dirty scenes that sprout in his mind. His collection is diverse, but it's gay love only. And if you are looking for something free, check his mailing list. Warning: it can be extra spicy.

When Michael Levi isn't writing, he's chilling out by the lake close to his house. Nothing better than kicking back with a martini in his hand as he daydreams his next explicit scenes.

Made in United States
Orlando, FL
04 March 2024